For Rafe
MB

For John
CR

First edition 2023

Library of Congress Catalog Card Number 2022908127
ISBN 978-1-5362-1513-7

22 23 24 25 26 27 CCP 10 9 8 7 6 5 4 3 2 1

Printed in Shenzhen, Guangdong, China

This book was typeset in Avenir.
The illustrations were done in mixed media.

Candlewick Press
99 Dover Street
Somerville, Massachusetts 02144

www.candlewick.com

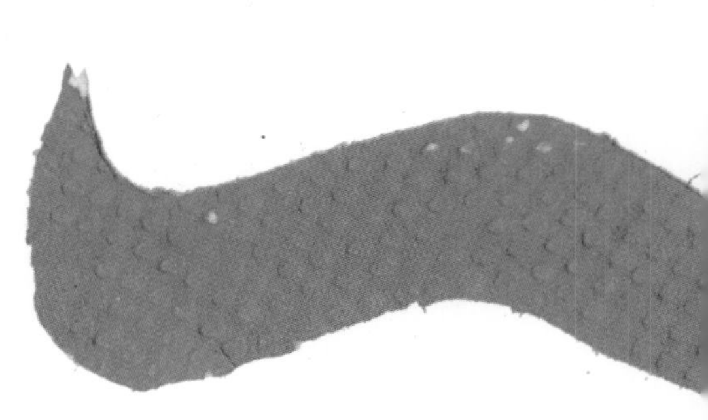

Mac Barnett   Christian Robinson

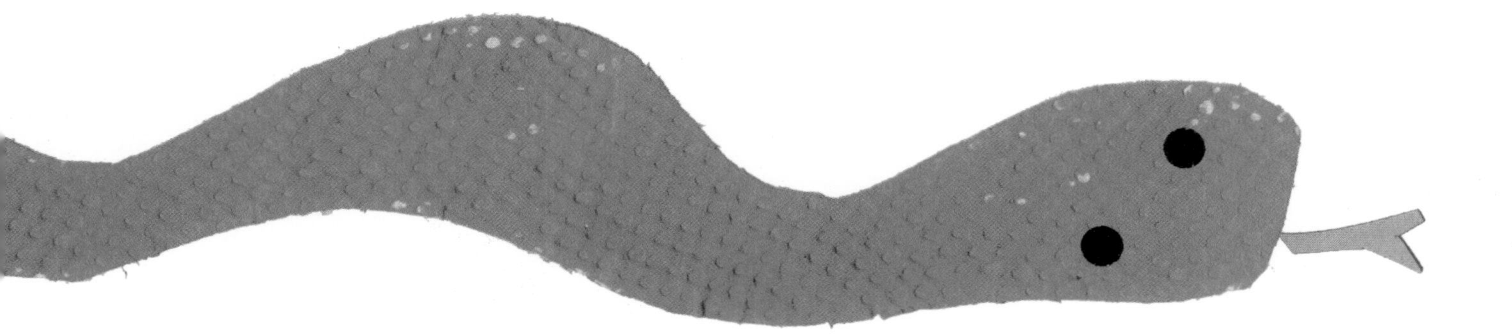

How many animals can you see in this picture?

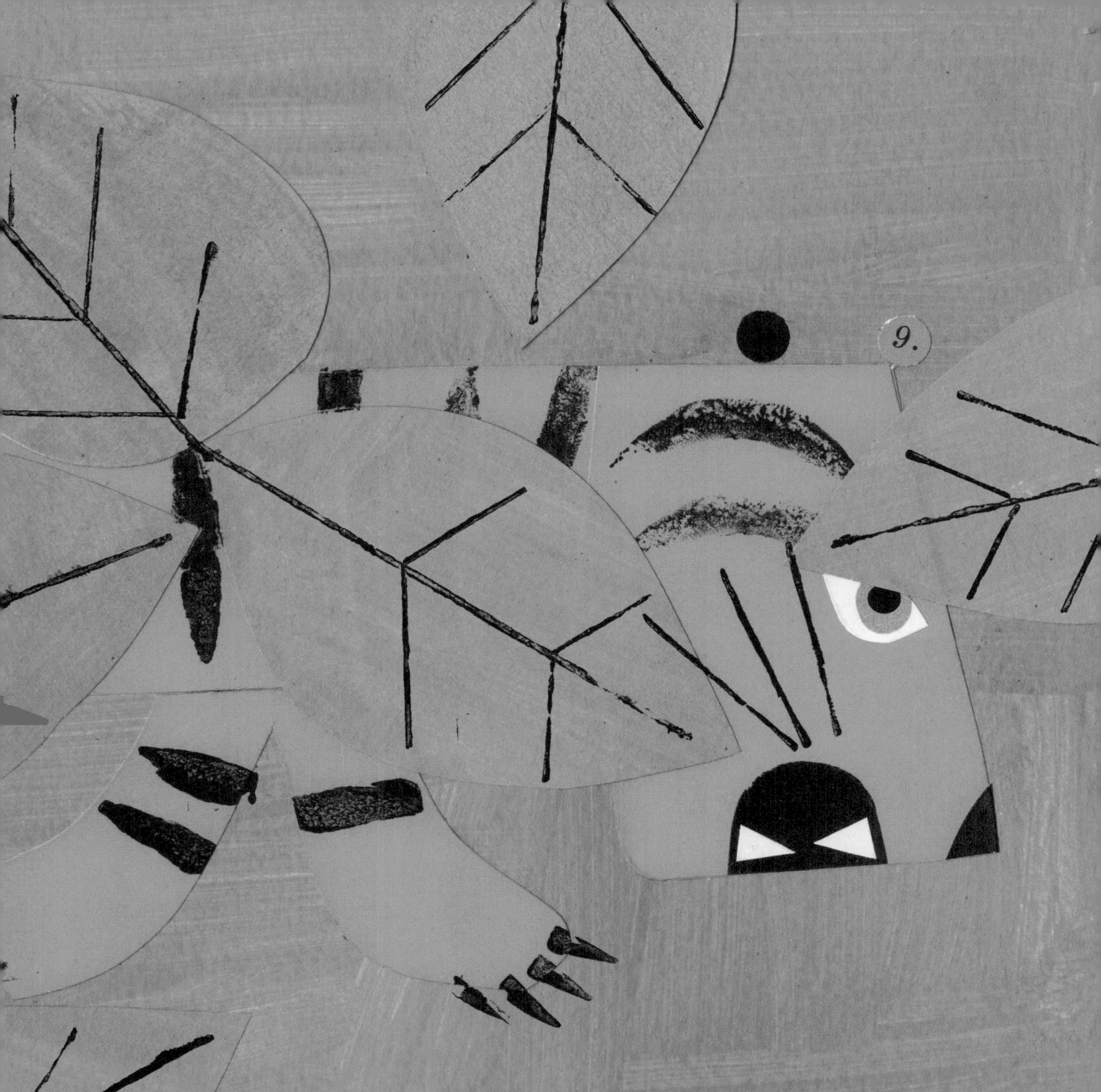

9.

How many animals can you not see in this one, because they're hiding from the tiger?

Which of these ladies just robbed a bank?

Why is the elephant so upset?

What is this boy hiding behind his back?

How did that cow get all the way up there?

Where did the bandits
bury the treasure?

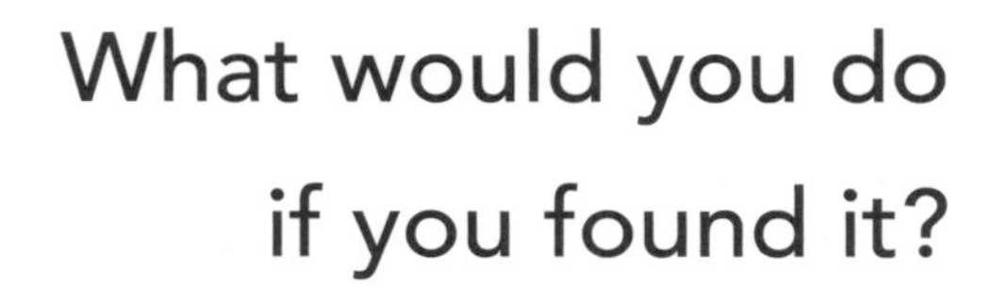

What would you do
if you found it?

Which
of these
creatures
is the
zookeeper's
favorite?

Who gave Mr. Beckett
a bump on his noggin?

What did the lion
get the lamb
for her birthday?

Who is she waiting for?

Which of these fellows has a better singing voice?

What
kind of
beast
lives
in this
bathtub?

And what does it eat?

Who is on the other side of this door?

Which of these children is dreaming of peaches?

Where is this ship sailing away to?

Will you go with it?

Are you ever coming back?

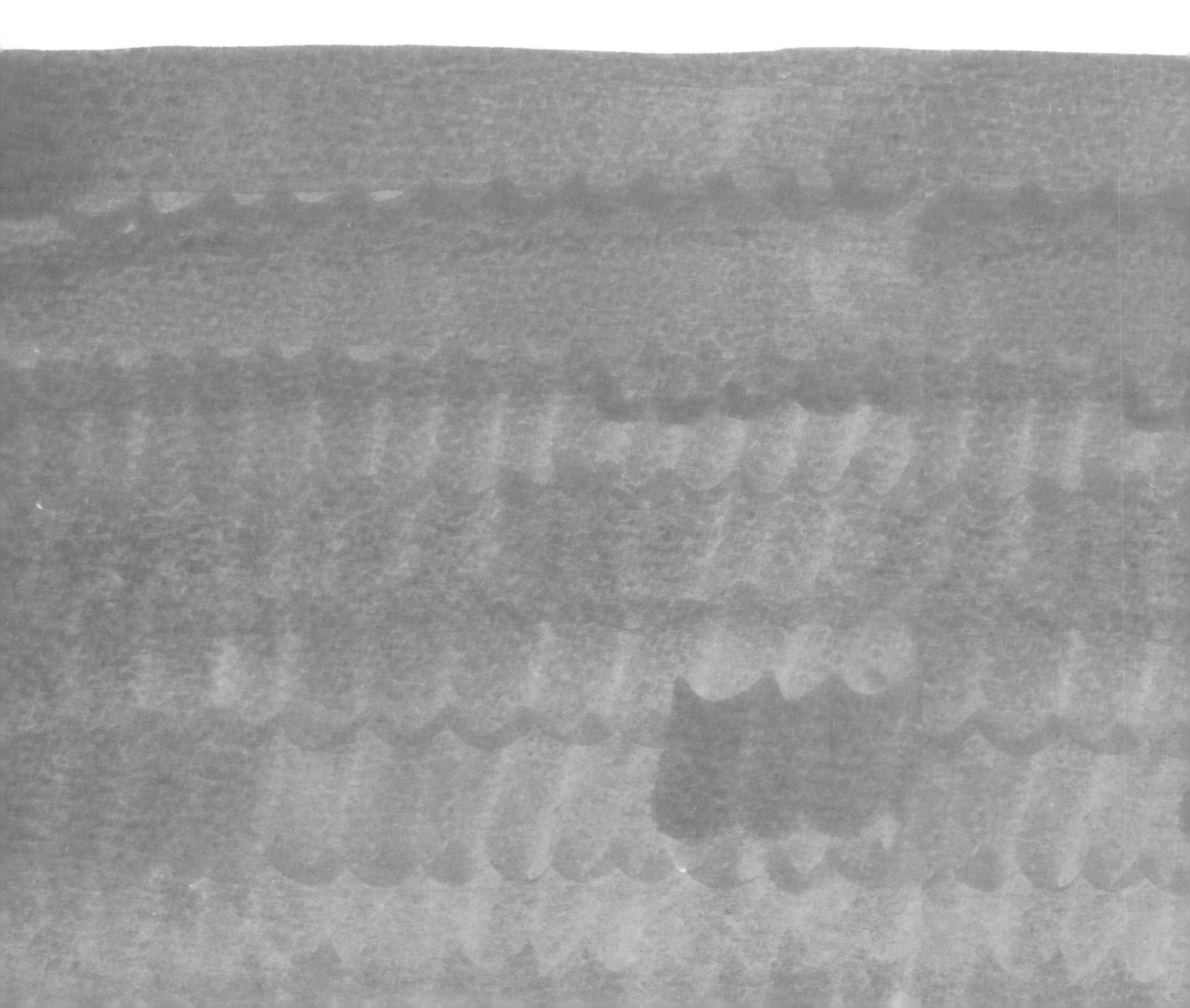

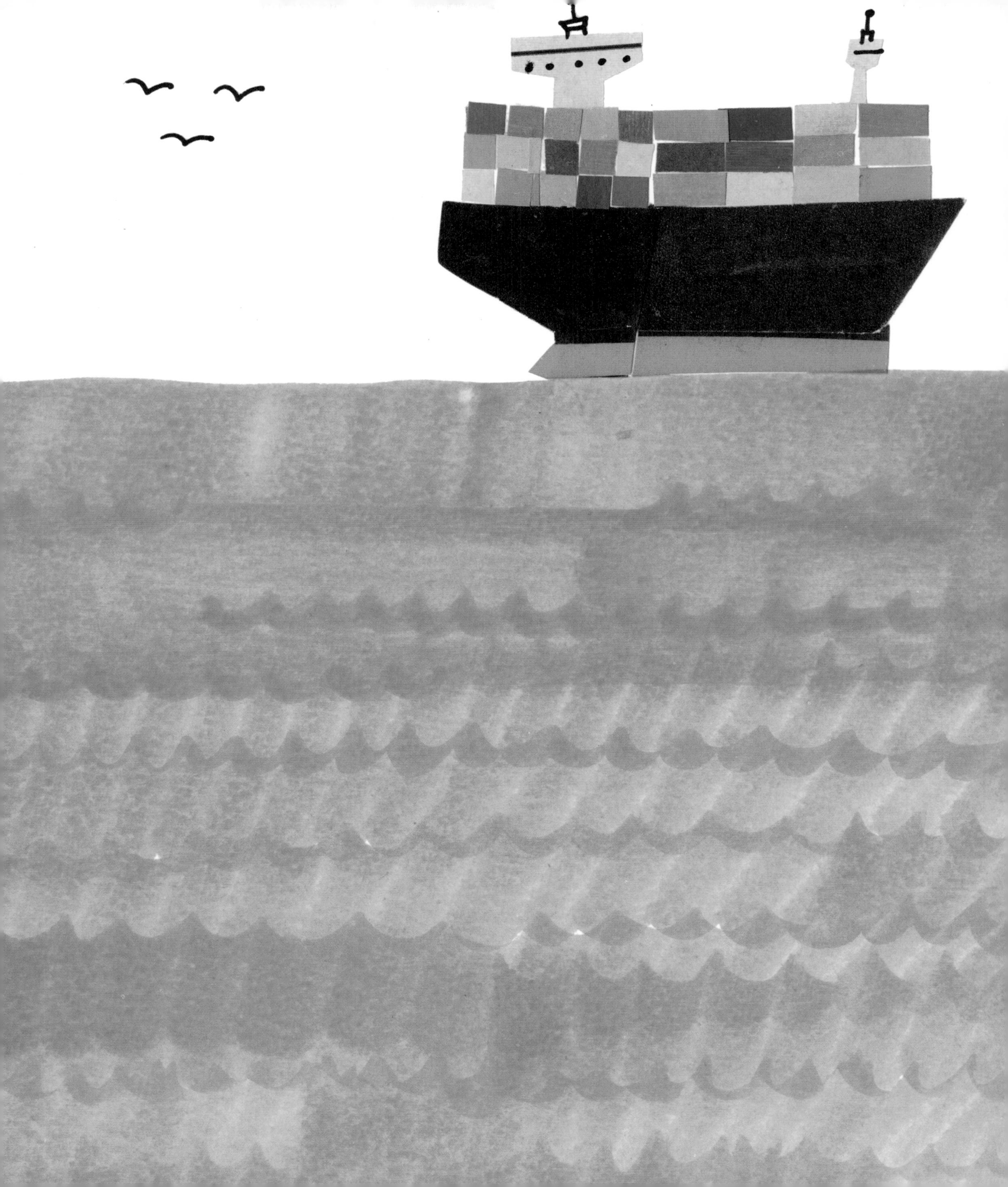